Young Cam Jansen
and the
Substitute Mystery

W9-APJ-023

BY DAVID A. ADLER
ILLUSTRATED BY SUSANNA NATTI

SCHOLASTIC INC.

New York Toronto London Auckland Sydney
Mexico City New Delhi Hong Kong Buenos Aires

To Mom and Dad Hamada
—D.A.

To Diana, Greg, and Hannah Rose
—S.N.

ISBN-13: 978-0-439-90628-9
ISBN-10: 0-439-90628-8

12 11 10 9 8 7 6 5 4   8 9 10 11 12/0

Printed in the U.S.A.   23

First Scholastic printing, January 2007

Set in Bookman

CONTENTS

1. Cam's Amazing Memory 4

2. The Square Egg 12

3. Cam Solves Mysteries 17

4. I Need My Coat 22

5. A Great Idea 26

A Cam Jansen Memory Game 31

1. CAM'S AMAZING MEMORY

Ms. Dee is out today

"Sit down! Sit down!"

Danny called out.

He was standing on Ms. Dee's desk.

"Ms. Dee is absent,

so I'm the teacher today."

Cam Jansen, her friend Eric Shelton,

and the others in Cam's class

did not sit down.

"Oh, so you won't sit down!"

Danny shouted.

"You're being punished.

I won't give you something.

I won't give you . . ." Danny said,

then thought for a moment.

"I won't give you homework!

That's what I won't give you."

"Hey," Tim said.

"Danny is a great teacher."

"Oh," a man said.

He was by the door to the class.

He had books, papers, and a lunch bag.

"I thought I was the teacher."

Danny jumped off the desk.

He hurried to his seat.

The others in the class

hurried to their seats, too.

"Is this Ms. Dee's class?" the man asked.

"Yes," Eric said.

The man walked in.

He dropped the books, papers,

and lunch bag on Ms. Dee's desk.

"I'm Mr. Baker," he told the class.

"I'm not a baker who bakes.

I'm a Baker who teaches.

Ms. Dee is absent,

so today I'm your teacher."

Mr. Baker sat in Ms. Dee's seat.

He looked through his papers.

"Oh, my," he said. "Ms. Dee left me a note,

but I can't find it."

Tim told Mr. Baker,

"There's a paper in your pocket.

Maybe it's the note."

Mr. Baker looked in his pants pockets

but didn't find the note.

"It's in your shirt pocket," Tim said.

"Oh, here it is," Mr. Baker said.

He opened the note and read it aloud.

"'I left math work for the class.

It's on the board.'"

Mr. Baker turned.

There was no math work

on the chalkboard.

"The custodian must have washed it,"
Eric said.

"Now what do I do?" Mr. Baker asked.

"We all saw it. Ms. Dee wrote it yesterday
afternoon, during silent reading," Eric said.

"Now you ask Cam to say, 'Click!'"

"'Click?' What's 'Click'?" Mr. Baker asked.

"Cam has an amazing memory," Eric said.

"She has a mental camera

with pictures in her head

of everything she's seen.

When she wants to remember something,

she just says, 'Click!'

That's the sound her mental camera makes."

Cam stood by the chalkboard.

She closed her eyes and said, "Click!"

She looked at the picture she had in her head.

Then she wrote all the math problems

Ms. Dee had written on the board.

Cam's real name is Jennifer,

but when people found out

about her great memory

they called her "The Camera."

Soon "The Camera" became just "Cam."

Mr. Baker looked at what Cam had written.

"You really do have

an amazing memory," he said.

2. THE SQUARE EGG

The children in Cam's class

copied the work from the chalkboard.

Danny didn't.

"What do I do next?" Danny asked.

"Next?" Mr. Baker asked.

"Have you done all the math work?"

"No," Danny answered. "I haven't done

any work. I just want to know

if there's something fun to do next."

"When you're done with the math work,"

Mr. Baker said, "you may read a book."

"I'll read a joke book," Danny said.

"That's fun."

Danny quickly copied the math problems.

"I'm done!" he said.

Eric turned and asked,

"You have answers to all the problems?"

"Sure, I have answers," Danny said.

"I have wrong answers.

I just wrote any number. I don't care.

Mr. Baker isn't our real teacher."

"Well, I care," Eric said.

"I want the right answers."

Danny opened his joke book.

"Hey," he asked Eric,

"what did the hen say

when she laid a square egg?"

"Sh!" Eric said.

"I'm trying to do my math problems."

"No," Danny told Eric.

"Why would a hen want to do math problems?

The hen said, 'Ouch!'

That's what the hen said."

"Oh," Eric said. "That's very interesting."

The children worked

on their math problems.

Then they read.

Ring! Ring!

It was the class telephone.

Mr. Baker picked it up.

"Hello," he said, and listened.

He put the telephone down

and told the class,

"That was Dr. Prell, the principal.

She said it's almost time for lunch.

We should take our coats.

After lunch, we're going outside to play."

"Yeah!" many of the children shouted.

"I'm going, too," Mr. Baker said.

Then he looked at the chair

beside Ms. Dee's desk.

"Oh my," he said.

"There's my lunch, but where's my coat?"

3. CAM SOLVES MYSTERIES

"Are you sure you wore a coat?"

Eric asked.

"Did I?" Mr. Baker asked himself.

"I drove here this morning.

Look, there's my car."

He pointed to a red car

in the school parking lot.

He checked his pockets.

"Look," he said.

He took everything from his pockets

and put it on Ms. Dee's desk.

"I have papers, bubble gum, pens,

coins, and a wallet," he said.

"I came in my car, but my car keys

and cell phone are not here.

I must have left them in my coat pockets."

Cam said, "Maybe you left

your coat in your car."

"Maybe I did!" Mr. Baker said.

He hurried to the telephone.

He called Dr. Prell.

He asked her to send someone

to watch the class.

A few minutes later

Mr. Day, the gym teacher,

walked into the room.

"I'm sorry," Mr. Baker told Mr. Day.

"I forgot where I left my coat.

I'll be right back," he told the class.

Cam watched through the window.

She saw Mr. Baker go outside.

He tried to open the door of his car,

but the doors were locked.

Mr. Baker looked through the car windows.

Then he walked back inside.

"My coat is not in my car," he told the class.

"Now what do I do?" Mr. Baker asked.

"Now you ask Cam to help you,"

Mr. Day said.

"Cam clicks and solves mysteries."

Cam closed her eyes and said, "Click!"

She said, "Click!" again.

Then Cam opened her eyes.

"This time clicking won't help," Cam said.

"I never saw Mr. Baker's coat."

"That's too bad," Mr. Day said.

"I'd like to stay and help,

but I must get back to the gym."

Mr. Baker thanked Mr. Day.

Then Mr. Baker sat by Ms. Dee's desk.

He shook his head and asked,

"Now what do I do?"

4. I NEED MY COAT

"I need my coat," Mr. Baker said.

"It's cold outside. I need my keys, too."

"Maybe I can help," Eric said.

"We know you wore your coat to school.

You didn't bring it to class.

So you must have left it somewhere

between your car and this room."

"Where did you go," Cam asked,

"after you left your car?"

Mr. Baker went to the window.

He pointed to the path

by the side of the school.

"I walked there," he said. "I came into school

and went to the main office."

"That's it!" Eric said.

"You left your coat in the main office."

Mr. Baker called the main office.

He spoke with Dr. Prell.

Then he shook his head and told the class,

"That's not it.

I didn't leave my coat in the main office."

"You left the coat on your way

to this room," Eric said.

"Now we walk slowly to the main office,

and look for it."

"That's a good idea," Mr. Baker said.

He stood and said,

"Get your coats and lunches.

Then follow me."

Mr. Baker took his lunch bag.

The class got their coats and lunches

and followed Mr. Baker.

They looked, and didn't find Mr. Baker's coat.

Then Eric turned and looked for Cam.

"Where is she? Where's Cam?" he asked.

"Oh, no," Mr. Baker said. "First I lost my coat.

Now I lost one of the children."

"You didn't lose her," Danny said.

"She's standing over there

with her eyes closed."

Just then Cam clapped her hands.

"I just remembered something," Cam said.

"Now I know how to find Mr. Baker's coat."

5. A GREAT IDEA

"Did you click and remember

something you saw?" Eric asked.

"No," Cam said.

"I remembered something I heard."

Then Cam asked Mr. Baker,

"Did you say you have your keys

and your cell phone

in the pockets of your coat?"

"Yes," Mr. Baker answered.

"Let's call your cell phone.

If it's somewhere between here

and our classroom,

we'll hear the ringing."

"That's a great idea," Mr. Baker said.

"I'll use the office telephone."

Cam told her classmates

to spread out in the hall

and listen for the ringing.

Mr. Baker went to the office.

He called his cell phone.

Ring! Ring!

"I hear it! I hear it!" Danny said.

Mr. Baker came out of the office.

"It came from in there," Danny said.

He pointed to the door

of the teachers' room.

Mr. Baker hurried to the teachers' room.

Cam and the other children did, too.

Mr. Baker opened the door.

There was a green coat on the couch.

"I forgot," Mr. Baker said.

"I came here this morning

before I went to class."

"I'm the one who found your coat,"

Danny said.

"Thank you," Mr. Baker said to Danny.

"Thank you, too," he said to Cam.

"You remember things you see

and things you hear.

You really are amazing."

Mr. Baker opened his lunch bag.

"I wonder what I have for lunch."

Then Mr. Baker laughed.

"I prepared my lunch and I forgot what it is!

Oh, I wish I had a Click! Click! memory."

He looked in his lunch bag and said,

"I wish I had a dessert, too."

The children in Ms. Dee's class ate lunch.

They shared their desserts with Mr. Baker.

Then they went outside to play.

Cam Jansen has an amazing memory. Do you?

Look at this picture. Blink your eyes and say, "Click!" Then turn the page.

A Cam Jansen
Memory Game

Take another look at the picture on page 31.

Study it.

Blink your eyes and say, "Click!"

Then turn back to this page

and answer these questions:

1. What color is Cam's jacket?

2. Who is on the jungle gym?

3. Where is Mr. Baker?

4. Is there a seesaw in the playground?

5. How many people are on the swings?